First published in 2007
by Hodder Children's Books.

Copyright © Mick Inkpen 2007

Hodder Children's Books
338 Euston Road, London, NW1 3BH

Hodder Children's Books Australia
Level 17/207 Kent Street, Sydney, NSW 2000

The right of Mick Inkpen to be identified as the author
and illustrator of this Work has been asserted by him in
accordance with the Copyright, Designs and Patents Act 1988.

A catalogue record of this book is
available from the British Library.

ISBN: 978 0 340 95997 8
10 9 8 7 6 5 4 3 2 1

Printed in China

Hodder Children's Books is a
division of Hachette Children's Books
An Hachette Livre UK Company

www.hachettelivre.co.uk

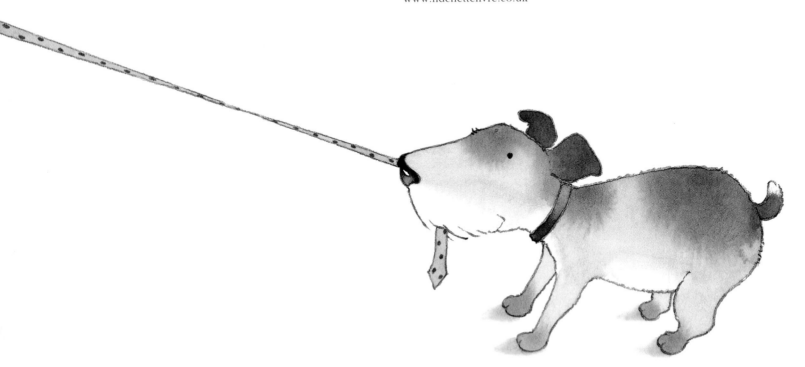

We are wearing out
the naughty step

Mick Inkpen

Hodder
Children's
Books

A division of Hachette Children's Books

'DON'T!'

Our dog thinks that its name is Don't! That's what Mummy is always saying to him.

But that's not his name.

His name is Angel.

It's not a good name for him.

He's not an angel.

He's naughty,

just like me. . .

. . .and my brother Josh, and my baby brother, Jimbo.

I've got my own Special Naughty Step. I sit quietly for two minutes until I am ready to say sorry.

I'm getting good at it. Kevin says so.

Josh's naughty step isn't a step at all. It's just a cushion on the floor! That's not a proper naughty step!

Today we are on our naughty steps because. . .

we have made Angel into a panda.

Last week at the zoo we were supposed to feed the elephant with the stuff in the white cups. That's the proper elephant stuff.

'JOSH, DON'T YOU DARE!'

But he did!

He really did!

He gave the elephant his chocolate!

Mummy says it isn't funny, but it is really, even though it is serious for elephants.

Mummy didn't want us to have the nursery hamster this weekend.

But I asked and asked and asked and asked and asked until she said I could have him.

'But ONLY if you don't get him out!'

I had to get him out, because he wanted me to so much.

Now I have to stay on my naughty step until Mummy finds him.

'If you don't eat your carrots like Josh you can't have any ice cream.' That's what Mummy says to me.

Sometimes I have to finish my carrots on the naughty step.

Kevin says carrots make you see in the dark, but I tried it and they don't work.

Sometimes I get ice cream without eating my carrots.

My bear Bertie has always had something fidgety inside him.

I wanted to see what it was. It was beans! Real beans!

I didn't mean them ALL to come out.

And it wasn't me that put one in Jimbo's ear.

On Tuesdays
Mummy gets ready
for her class.
She's nearly
always late.
She's always in
a hurry.

Ding! Dong!
'Be GOOD for the new babysitter!'
She rushed to the door and slipped on a bean from Bertie.
'Ouch!
Ouch!
Ouch!'

She had to miss her class. And then she cried.

'Today is Kevin's birthday.
So today is a good day to be good.'

We managed to be good all day.
It was Angel that spoilt it.
He jumped up and licked Kevin's
special cake.
And when I tried to mend it
I accidentally licked my fingers.
And Josh said it was only fair
if he could lick some too. . .

And that was when Mummy
came in. And even though it was
Kevin's cake she said,

'My cake!'

very loudly.

And then very quietly she said,
'That's it! That's really it!'
And her words went
sort of wobbly.

'I have reached the end of my **TETHER!**'

And after she reached the end of her tether,
that's when she did the amazing thing. . .

She grabbed a really big handful of cake and squeezed it between her fingers! Then she tipped all the shiny little balls over it and squidged it into her mouth!

She did!

She really, really did!

All of it!

All in one go!

And then she stopped.

And everything went quiet.

And Jimbo was the first one
to make a sound.

It was his first word.
(It really was.)

'Did he say "Cake?"' said Josh.

'He did!' I said.
'He said, "Cake!"'

And then Mummy laughed.
And we laughed too.
I think it was Jimbo saying,
'Cake!' that made her feel better.
Or it might have been
the chocolate.

Anyway we laughed
for ages. And when
Angel had licked the
chocolate off us,
Mummy said,
    'I suppose I should
sit on the naughty step!'
which made us laugh
some more.
    And I said
'You can borrow
mine!'

And we made her do it.

We got a book and
we all sat on the naughty
step, Mummy and Josh
and Jimbo and Angel and
Bertie and me.
 And when Kevin came
round we let him sit on
the naughty step with us.
 (I think Mummy
 likes Kevin.)

 And Kevin said,
'So! We are all
naughty!'
 And I said,
'We are all nice.'